go Cow___ys!

Dallas Cowboys
Coloring & Activity Storybook

by Brad M. Epstein
illustrations by Curt Walstead

michaelson entertainment

Aliso Viejo, CA www.michaelsonentertainment.com
Designed in California

ISBN-13: 978-1-60730-508-8

Stadium for the big game.

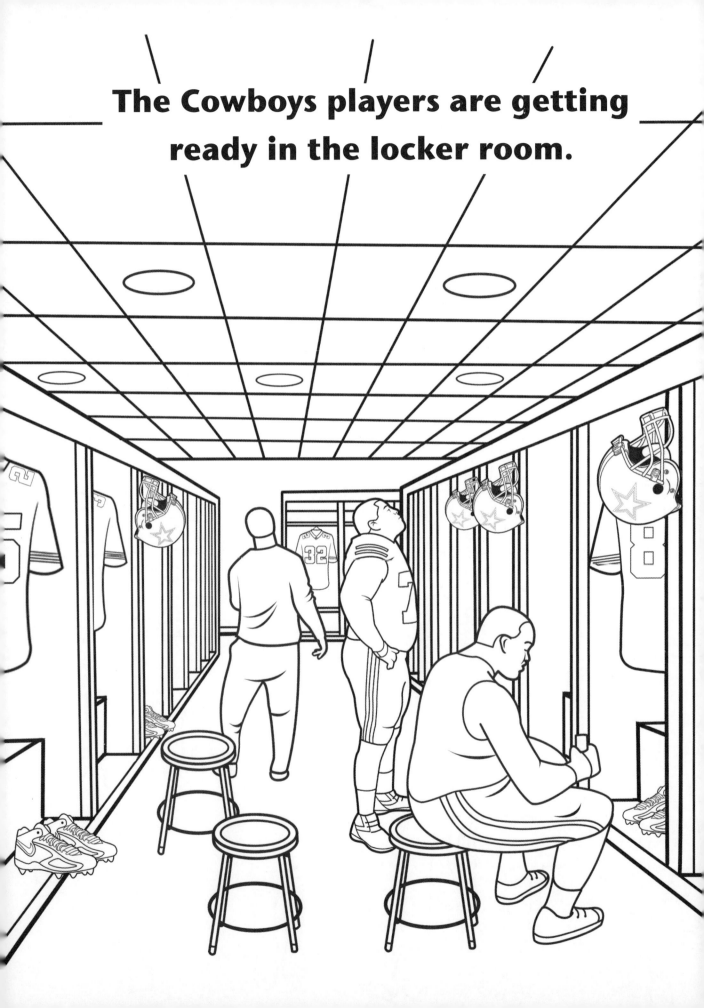

The Cowboys players are getting ready in the locker room.

Help the players get into their uniforms.

Unscramble the words.

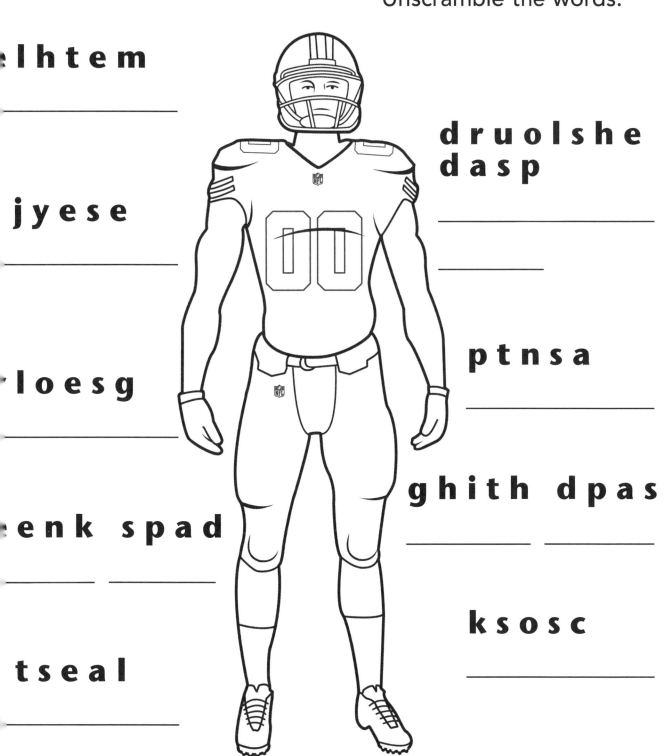

lhtem

_____

jyese

_____

loesg

_____

enk spad

_____

tseal

_____

druolshe dasp

_____

ptnsa

_____

ghith dpas

_____

ksosc

_____

The Cowboys take the field!

Here's a close-up of the Cowboys jersey

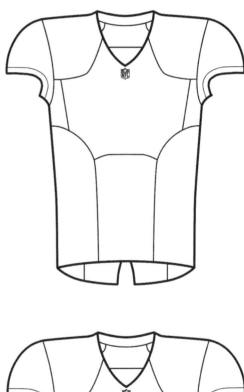

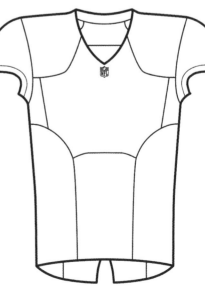

Color it in,
then create your own jersey designs.

kickoff

Our **kicker** **kicks the ball.**

The Cowboys **defense** stops the Redskins in 4 downs.

the Cowboys are awesome!

```
E N S T I I V X X X X Q
H A I L M A R Y X O X D
C V L A N D C V E B I A
A Y V L I O I N T A C L
B N E Q W I R O W D Y L
U I R B I O U Z S I L A
A V O W O C B A C A R S
T Y J L H O X R O W W D
S R E D A E L R E E H C
U O O X T M A R Y P H E
P W K I F T Z U B V U A
N D R I S A F H T I M S
```

Word Search:
Find the Dallas Cowboys football words in this list.

Cheerleaders	Navy	Star
Cowboys	Rowdy	Staubach
Dallas	Silver	Super Bowl
Hail Mary	Smith	Touchdown

timeout: find the Cowboys Super Bowl championships (VI, XII, XXVII, XXVIII,XXX)

The Cowboys **offense** is on the field. It's first and ten at the twenty yard line.

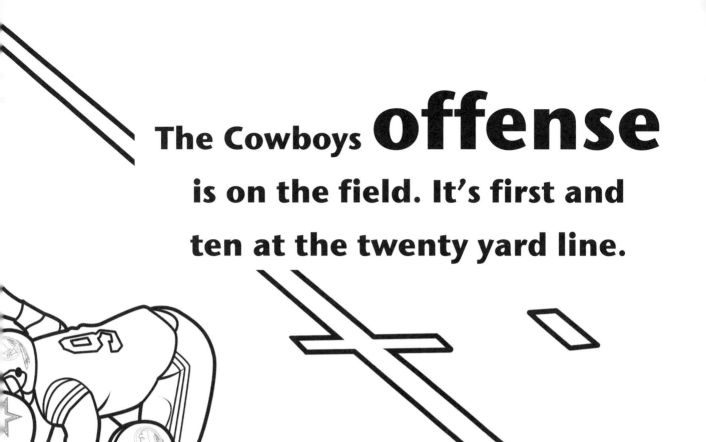

The

quarterback

fades back to pass.

Help the Cowboys quarterback throw a
complete pass.

throw

(start)

(finish)

catch

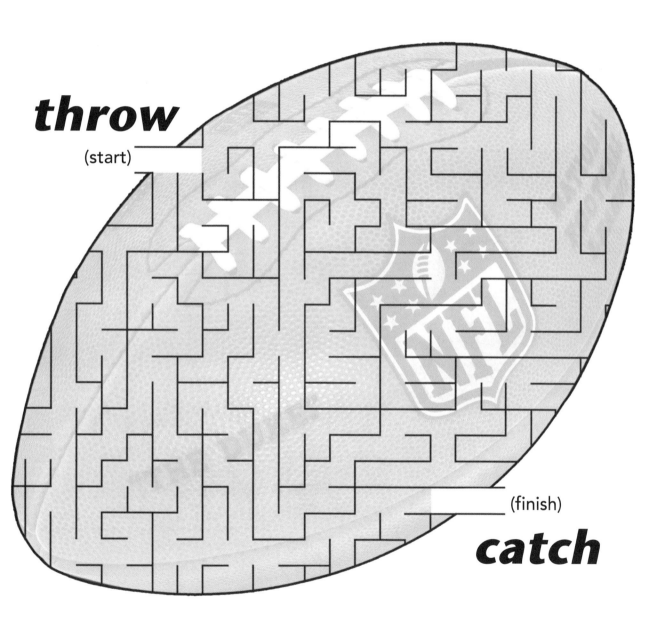

Find a path from the quarterback's
throw to the wide receiver's catch.

The **wide receiver** makes a spectacular leaping catch!

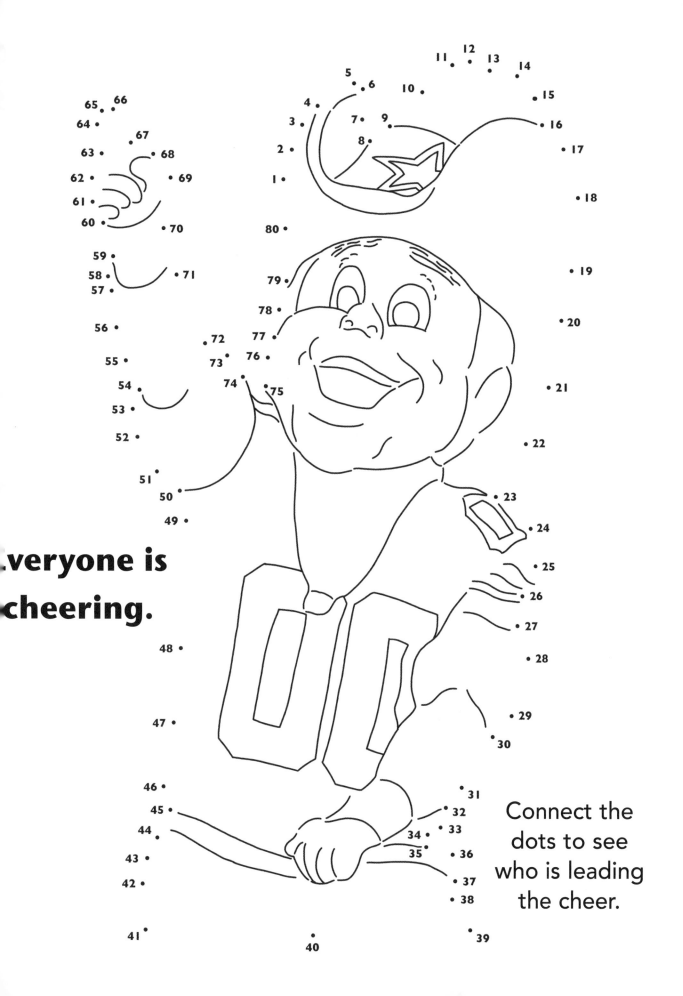

Everyone is cheering.

Connect the dots to see who is leading the cheer.

It's 2nd down. Make sure the players are in their correct positions.

```
N C E N T E R R A H S W
G U O Z O Y T E F A S E
U T R R O R E T D L A C
A V E E N L M N Q F P O
R E K S K E E U U B R Z
D A C C N L R P V A E O
Q U A R T E R B A C K H
A T B T O O F X A K C H
N R E V I E C E R C I C
E S N E F F O Q D A K A
O D I Z M A N A G E R O
C A L K C A B L L U F C
```

Word Search: Find the names of the players and their positions in this list.

Cornerback	**Guard**	**Punter**
Center	**Halfback**	**Quarterback**
Defense	**Kicker**	**Receiver**
End	**Linebacker**	**Safety**
Fullback	**Offense**	**Tackle**

Huddle Up

It's a handoff, and...

...the Cowboys sta[r]

running bac[k]

breaks a tackle... and runs into the end zone!

TOUCHDOWN!

How many points are earned for each scoring play?

Unscramble the words, then match the scoring play to the correct number of points.

fastye

_____

2

eaxrt ipotn

_____ _____

6

chodtuwno

_____

3

fleid loag

_____ _____

1

Instant Replay!

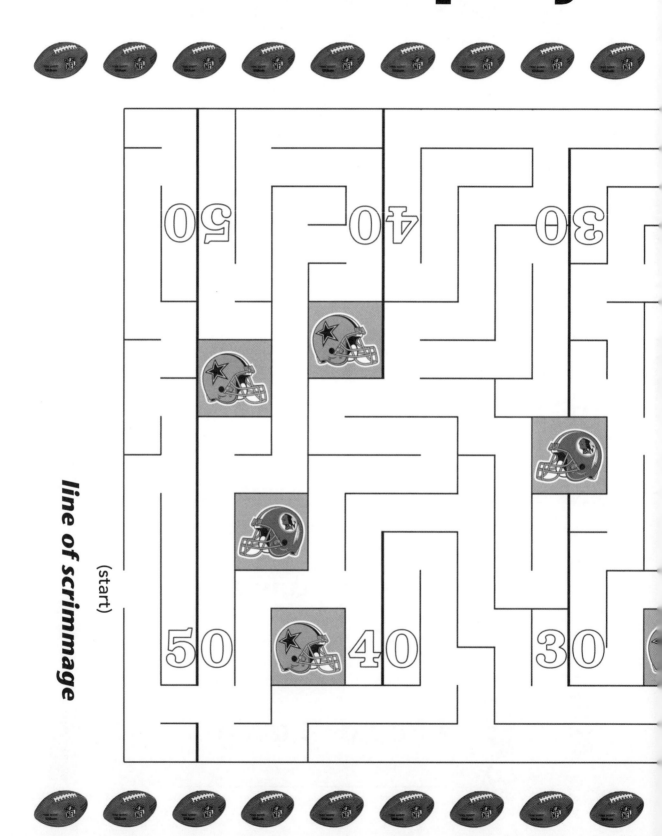

line of scrimmage

(start)

Let's see how the running back scored the touchdown.
Find a path from the line of scrimmage to the end zone.
(don't get 'tackled' by the Washington Redskins helmets)

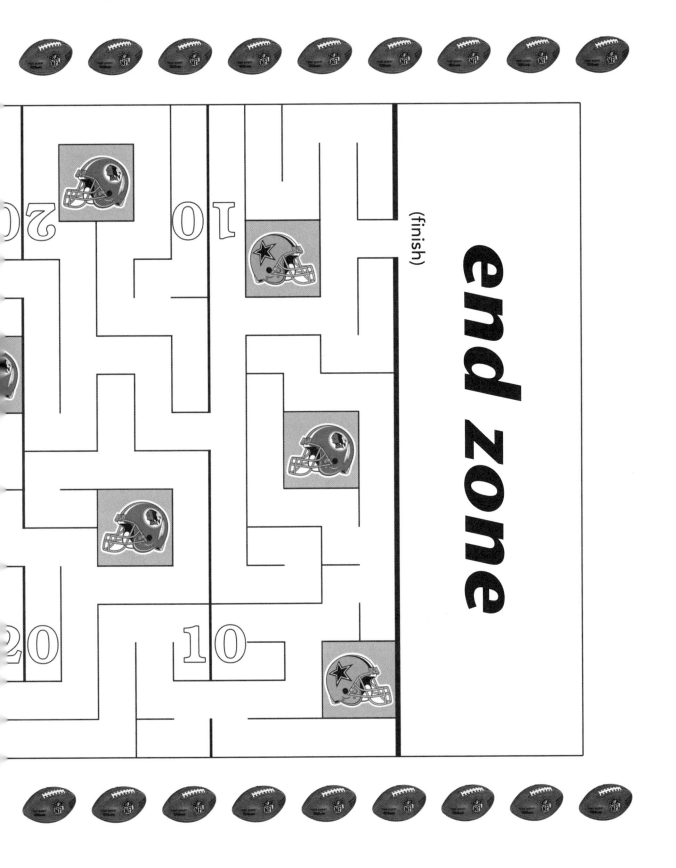

All of the **Dallas Cowboys**

Color in the stadium, draw some fans too.

fans are on their feet,

cheering in **AT&T Stadium.**

Let's put a **Cowboys logo** on the 50-yard line of the field.

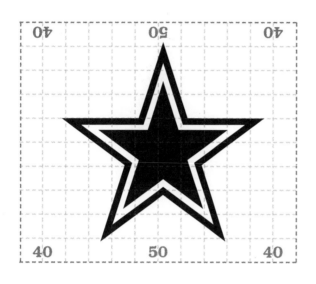

Use the grid as a guide to draw a big Dallas Cowboys logo on the 'field' below. We've started with the top left corner.

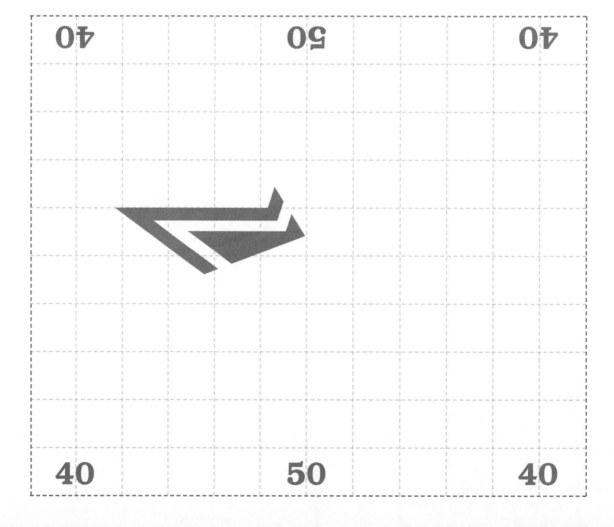

it's halftime

What does every Cowboys fan know? Solve the message by using the secret code below.

T H E

C O W B O Y S

A R E T H E

G R E A T E S T

 = A   = G   = S

 = B   = H   = T

 = C   = O   = W

 = E   = R   = Y

enter the

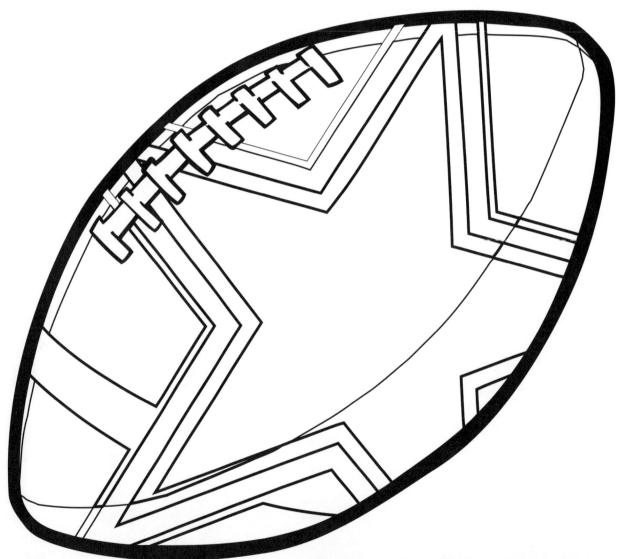

color in the Cowboys
megacore

Help protect the home team in the Rush Zone!

Word Search: Find the names of these things in the Rush Zone.

Blitz Bot	**Guardian**	**Ohio**
Canton	**Hall of Fame**	**Rusher**
Drop Kick	**Ish**	**Teamland**
Football	**Megacore**	**Wild Card**

Watch out for imposters!

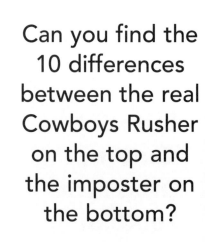

Can you find the 10 differences between the real Cowboys Rusher on the top and the imposter on the bottom?

Cowboys Rusher

The **2nd half** is about to start.
Make some noise!

Color in the Cowboys logo

The **center** snaps the ball to start the play...

Rowdy

is on the sideline, cheering for our team!

great
tackle

Our
defense
is on
the field.

Play by Play

It is a close game but our team is behind by 2 points.
You are the coach. Can you tell our players what to do?
(circle the correct answers)

Our
coach
defense
offense
needs to stop the Redskins' offense.

....

Then we need to recover a
fumble
tackle
touchdown
or we need to

force an
interception
pass
penalty
to take possession.

....

Our offense will need to score at least
two
three
four
points to take the lead.

....

We need to score a
extra point
field goal
first down
or a
block
punt
touchdown
to win.

It's 4th down, we need a
field goal to win the game.

It's long enough,
it's good.
SCORE!

Instant Replay!

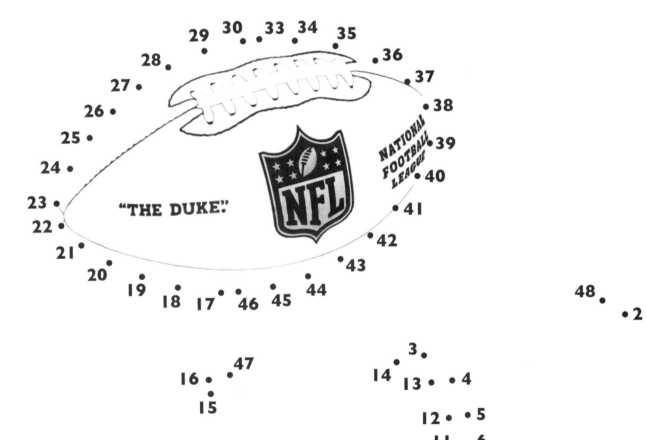

Connect the dots to see a
close-up of the field goal.

The Cowboys win!

What is the goal of every player? Solve the message by using the secret code below.

T

 = A	= I	= P	= U
= B	= L	 = R	 = W
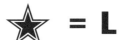 = E	= N	 = S	 = Y
 = H	 = O	= T	

If the Cowboys are the best team, we can

It will be difficult becaus[...]
There are 32 awesome tea[...]

Bengals _____

Bills __a__

Broncos _____

Browns _____

Chargers _____

Chiefs _____

Colts _____

Dolphins _____

Jaguars _____

Jets _____

Patriots _____

Raiders _____

Ravens _____

Steelers _____

Texans _____

Titans _____

Match each
(exam[...]

win the **Super Bowl**.

...e is a lot of competition.
...e National Football League.

Bears	_____
Buccaneers	_____
Cardinals	_____
Cowboys	_____
Eagles	_____
Falcons	_____
Forty Niners	_____
Giants	_____
Lions	_____
Packers	_____
Panthers	_____
Rams	_____
Redskins	_____
Saints	_____
Seahawks	_____
Vikings	_____

q   r   s   t

u   v   w   x

y   z   aa   bb

cc   dd   ee   ff

NATIONAL

...ith its logo.
...is 'a')

The game is over. It's time to go home.

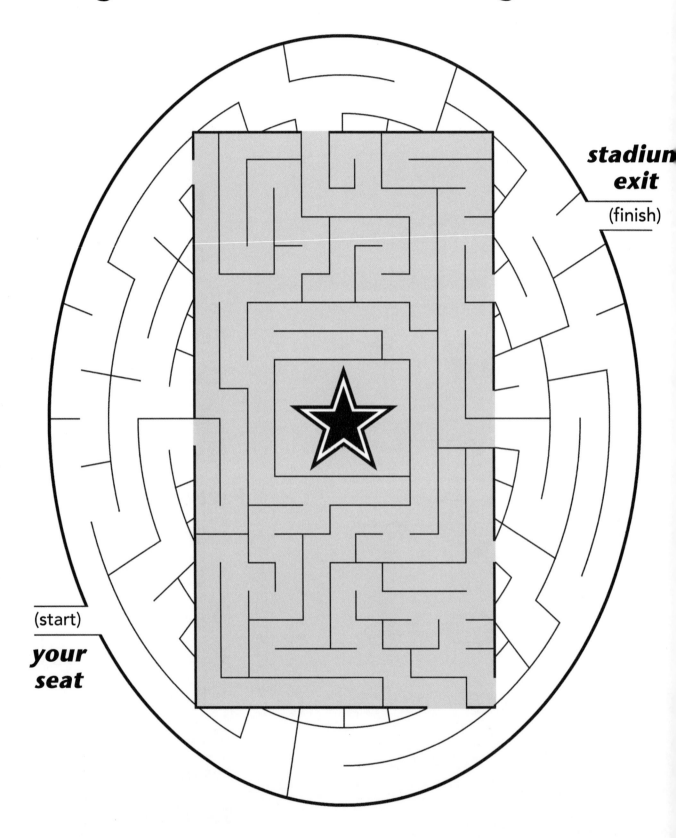

stadium exit

(finish)

(start)

your seat

Find a path from 'your seat' to the 'stadium exit.'

Let's draw the NFL logo.

Use the grid as a
guide to draw a
big NFL logo.
We've started with
the top left corner.

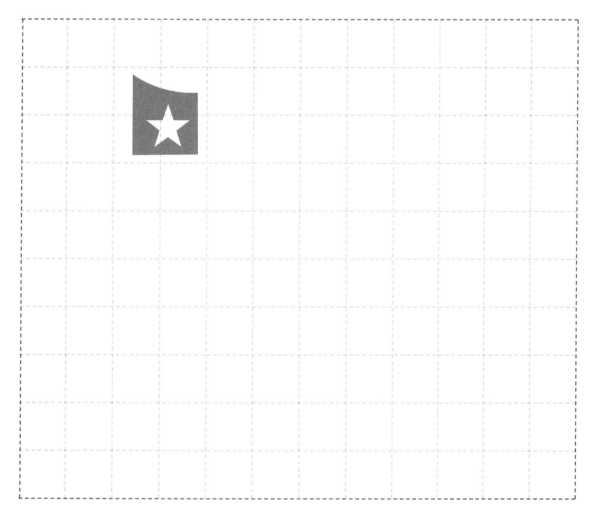

Solutions to Games and Puzzles

Page 5

Help the players get into their uniforms.

Unscramble the words.

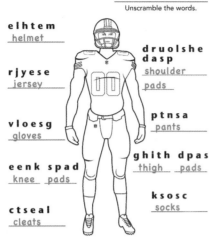

e l h t e m
helmet

r j y e s e
jersey

v l o e s g
gloves

e e n k s p a d
knee pads

c t s e a l
cleats

d r u o l s h e d a s p
shoulder pads

p t n s a
pants

g h i t h d p a s
thigh pads

k s o s c
socks

Page 11

the Cowboys are awesome!

Word Search:
Find the Dallas Cowboys football words in this list.

Cheerleaders	Navy	Star
Cowboys	Rowdy	Staubach
Dallas	Silver	Super Bowl
Hail Mary	Smith	Touchdown

timeout: find the Cowboys Super Bowl championships (VI, XII, XXVII, XXVIII, XXX)

Page 15

Help the Cowboys quarterback throw a complete pass.

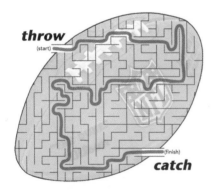

throw
(start)

(finish)
catch

Find a path from the quarterback's throw to the wide receiver's catch.

Page 17

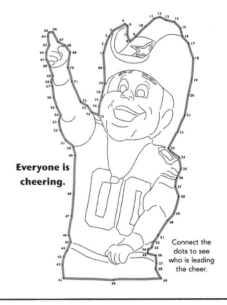

Everyone is cheering.

Connect the dots to see who is leading the cheer.

Page 18

It's 2nd down. Make sure the players are in their correct positions.

Word Search: Find the names of the players and their positions in this list.

Cornerback	Guard	Punter
Center	Halfback	Quarterback
Defense	Kicker	Receiver
End	Linebacker	Safety
Fullback	Offense	Tackle

Page 21

TOUCHDOWN!

How many points are earned for each scoring play?

Unscramble the words, then match the scoring play to the correct number of points.

f a s t y e
safety   **2**

e a x r t i p o t n
extra point   **6**

c h o d t u w n o
touchdown   **3**

f l e i d l o a g
field goal   **1**

Solutions to Games and Puzzles

Page 22-23

Instant Replay!

Let's see how the running back scored the touchdown. Find a path from the line of scrimmage to the end zone. (don't get 'tackled' by the Washington Redskins helmets)

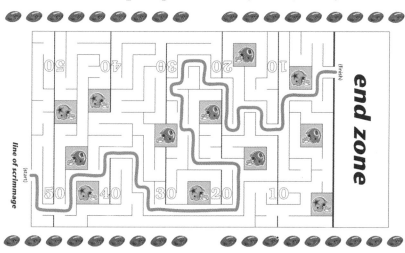

Page 27

it's halftime

What does every Cowboys fan know? Solve the message by using the secret code below.

T H E

C O W B O Y S

A R E T H E

G R E A T E S T

= A	= G	= S
= B	= H	= T
= C	= O	= W
= E	= R	= Y

Page 29

Help protect the home team in the Rush Zone!

```
I P T E L A N G P D O T
M E G A C O R E D R E C
L R R R T E A M L A N D
U F S N W O L A T C M W
L L A B T O O F R D W N
I C H R H A A F R L H D
L B L I T Z B O T I S Z
E B O S M N P L Q W U O
N M Z H D K E L H R R N
K F N A I D R A U G I E
R A L C O R E H S U R E
O K K H M R M I R S A K
```

Word Search: Find the names of these things in the Rush Zone.

Blitz Bot	**Guardian**	**Ohio**
Canton	**Hall of Fame**	**Rusher**
Drop Kick	**Ish**	**Teamland**
Football	**Megacore**	**Wild Card**

Page 30

Watch out for imposters!

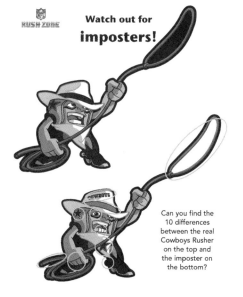

Can you find the 10 differences between the real Cowboys Rusher on the top and the imposter on the bottom?

Page 36

Play by Play

It is a close game but our team is behind by 2 points. You are the coach. Can you tell our players what to do? (circle the correct answers)

Our (defense) needs to stop the Redskins' offense.
(coach / defense / offense)

Then we need to recover a **tackle** *(fumble / tackle / touchdown)* or we need to

force an **pass** *(interception / pass / penalty)* to take possession.

Our offense will need to score at least (three) points to take the lead. *(two / three / four)*

We need to score a (field goal) *(extra point / field goal / first down)* or a **punt** *(block / punt / touchdown)* to win.

Solutions to Games and Puzzles

Page 39   Instant Replay!

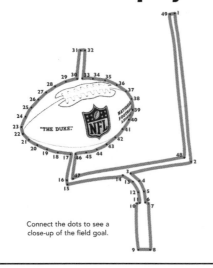

Connect the dots to see a close-up of the field goal.

Page 41   The Cowboys win!

What is the goal of every player? Solve the message by using the secret code below.

T O   P L A Y

I N   T H E

S U P E R

B O W L

= A	= I	= P	= U
= B	= L	= R	= W
= E	= N	= S	= Y
= H	= O	= T	

Page 42-43

If the Cowboys are the best team, we can win the **Super Bowl.**

It will be difficult because there is a lot of competition.
There are 32 awesome teams in the National Football League.

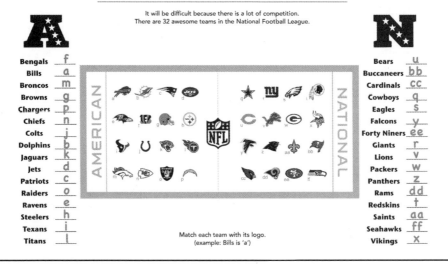

Match each team with its logo.
(example: Bills is 'a')

AMERICAN		NATIONAL	
Bengals	f	Bears	u
Bills	a	Buccaneers	bb
Broncos	m	Cardinals	cc
Browns	g	Cowboys	q
Chargers	p	Eagles	s
Chiefs	n	Falcons	y
Colts	j	Forty Niners	ee
Dolphins	b	Giants	r
Jaguars	k	Lions	v
Jets	d	Packers	w
Patriots	c	Panthers	z
Raiders	o	Rams	dd
Ravens	e	Redskins	t
Steelers	h	Saints	aa
Texans	i	Seahawks	ff
Titans	l	Vikings	x

Page 44

The game is over. It's time to go home.

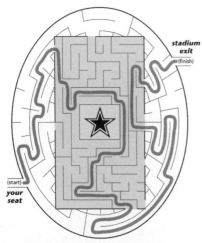

Find a path from 'your seat' to the 'stadium exit.'